Let's Play Tag!

🔖 Read the Page

▶ Read the Story

⭐ Game

😊 Yes   😞 No

🔄 Repeat

⏹ Stop

Up With Adventure

illustrated by Lee Cosgrove

Our uplifting adventure begins with an unlikely hero named Carl Fredricksen.

Carl was a retired balloon salesman who had a goal—to visit Paradise Falls in South America. So one day, having tied thousands of balloons to his house, Carl set sail into the sky.

But he wasn't alone! There was a stowaway on board— a Junior Wilderness Explorer named Russell. Russell wanted to earn his Assisting the Elderly merit badge.

4

After a bumpy flight through a storm,
Carl and Russell finally landed the house
in South America!

But they still had a long way to travel before
they would reach Paradise Falls.

Carl and Russell trekked through the jungle toward the falls, pulling the house behind them.

"This is fun already, isn't it?" said Russell, hopefully.

But it wasn't. Lugging the big house turned out to be hard work!

Russell grew tired and looked for a place to rest. Instead, he found some tracks in the dirt. He followed the tracks to the biggest, most beautiful bird he had ever seen!

Russell named the bird Kevin.

"Can we keep him? Please?" Russell asked Carl.

Carl said no.

"Shoo!" Carl said to the bird.

Russell didn't want to leave Kevin behind.
So when Carl wasn't looking, Russell left a trail
of chocolates for the bird to follow. The bird loved
to eat chocolate!

Latin name of Cocoa Tree—
Theobroma cacao

Before long, Carl and Russell came across some twisty rocks.

"That one looks like a dog!" Russell said, pointing at a rock.

The rock walked forward. It wasn't a rock at all! It really was a dog.

"Hi there," said the dog. "My name is Dug."

It was a talking dog!

Dug's master had sent Dug's pack to look for a rare bird.

"Hey, that is the bird!" said Dug. "She has been separated from her babies by my pack."

Kevin was a girl? They had to help Kevin get back to her babies!

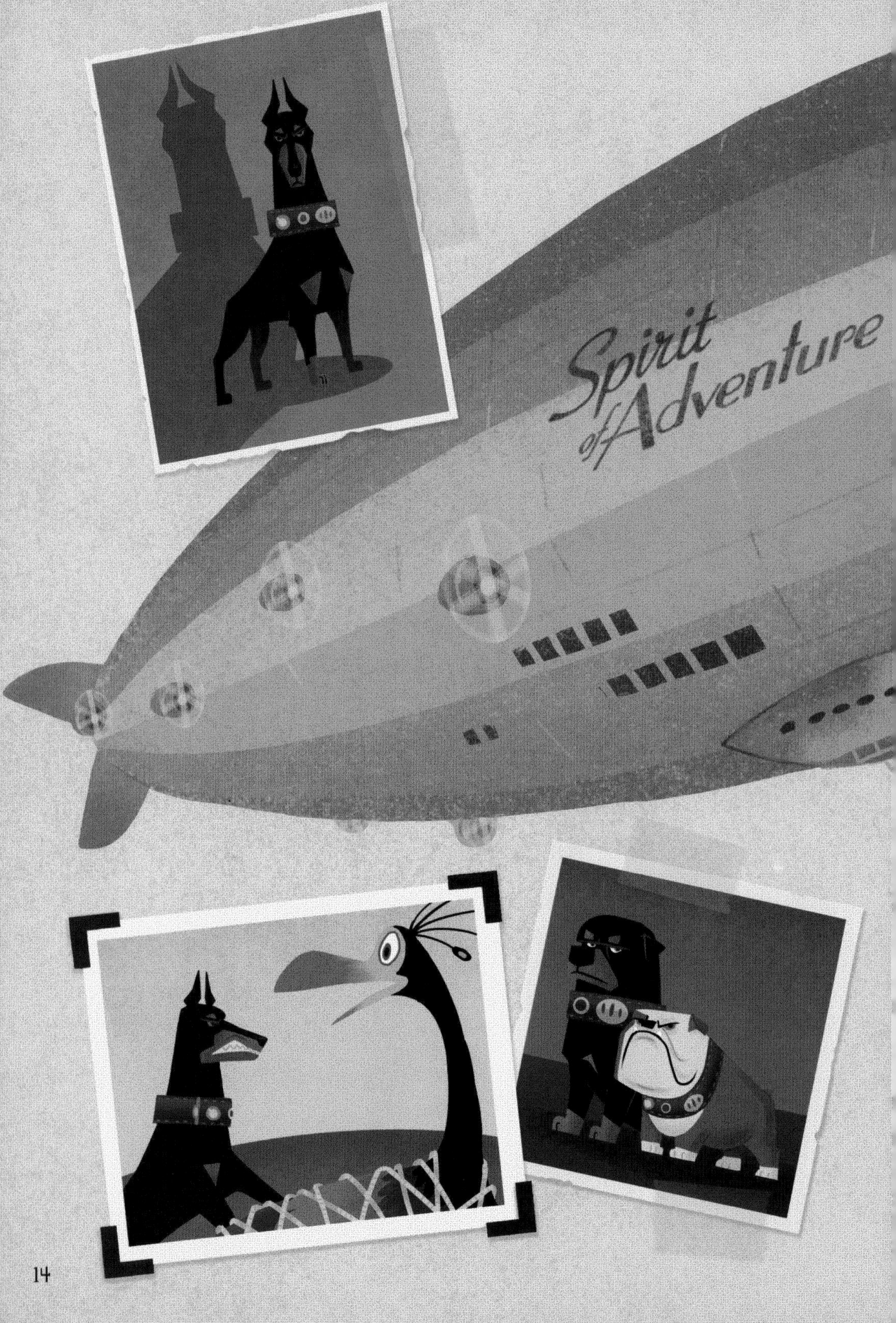
Spirit of Adventure

Adventure is Out There!

The beloved aviation pioneer Charles F. Muntz lands his dirigible, the Spirit of Adventure, in New Hampshire this week, completing a year long expedition to the lost world!

Just then, Dug's master, the famous explorer Charles F. Muntz, and the other dogs in Dug's pack arrived. Alpha, Beta, and Gamma weren't nice dogs like Dug. They grabbed Kevin, and took her into their dirigible.

Carl was ready to give up. He was no match for Muntz and the pack of dogs. He would continue on to Paradise Falls without Kevin.

But not Russell. "An explorer is a friend to all, be it plants or fish or tiny mole!" he said.

Russell grabbed some balloons and used a leaf blower to soar up into the sky. "I'm going to help Kevin, even if you won't!" he shouted to Carl down below as he flew off after the dirigible.

Carl and Dug couldn't let Russell go alone!
They flew the house up to Muntz's dirigible.

It looked like their rescue was going to work.

Rope Climbing Techniques

Elective 17

When climbing a rope, don't forget about your legs! You can use your leg strength to help pull yourself up the rope.

Until Muntz's dogs whooshed down in fighter planes!

Carl, Dug, and Russell had to work fast. They found
Kevin and made a daring escape!

Next stop: Kevin's home among the twisty rocks.

Kevin's babies were overjoyed to see her. Carl was happy, too. The trip hadn't been quite what he'd expected, but he wouldn't trade it for anything. And Russell was happy. He would finally earn his —Assisting the Elderly merit badge!

It was an expedition Carl and Russell would remember forever—one that taught them the true spirit of adventure.

Amazon Explorers